Once Upon a Winter Solstice

An Enchanted Highlands Novella

By: Victoria Zak

Copyright

Once Upon a Winter Solstice
Victoria Zak

Copyright © Victoria Zak, 2015

Cover Design by JAB Designs

Editing by Kathryn Lynn Davis and Julie Roberts

ISBN: 978-1-942516-16-3

Contents

Dedication

What if all moments throughout time existed at once? What if you had a love that stood the test of time? Never faltering, never fading. What if one legend brought both time and love together as one? Once Upon a Winter Solstice is dedicated to those who believe in true love. Enjoy!

Victoria Zak

Chapter One

Highland Falls, NY

December 20, present day

"Are you sure you can lock up by yourself, Ivy? I don't mind staying."

"Yes," Ivy reassured her best friend and co-owner of the Highland Falls Art Gallery. "I'll be fine." Ivy helped her friend into her woolen winter coat and ushered her to the front door. "Besides, Dean is waiting outside for you."

Poppy Sinclair's better half had made it known several times over the past five minutes that he had grown impatient with her by blaring the horn from inside his silver SRL McLaren parked curbside.

Ivy rolled her eyes and opened the door to the art gallery. A bitter chill blew through her little black dress, causing her to shiver.

"Poppy!" Dean called out of the rolled-down window. "Get your ass in the car. We're going to be late."

"Hi, Dean." Ivy waved and did her best to smile. There was no doubt about it, Dean was the kind of man who didn't like to be kept waiting. He was a high-profile lawyer who worked and lived on the upper east side of

1

Manhattan; driving an hour and twenty minutes to Highland Falls on the coldest day of the year had put him in a foul mood.

It was Poppy and Ivy's last art exhibit for the year; he should cut Poppy some slack and be happy for her: the event had been a huge success. Throughout the occasion he'd mingled when it mattered the most, beaming at Poppy as a journalist from the local news station interviewed her and praised her for her paintings. Ivy knew better than to believe the façade, and had to bite her tongue and grab a glass of wine as the waiter passed by. She had needed something to wash the bile down as she watched him eye his Rolex and exhale in frustration. The man was truly an arrogant ass. What Poppy saw in him Ivy would never know.

Dean smiled back at Ivy. "Hey, are you still seeing that guy…"

"Mark?"

Dean snapped his fingers. "Yes, him."

Ivy rubbed her hands up and down her arms, trying to ward off the cold and, before she could answer, Poppy stepped out of the gallery and reached for the car handle. "Dean, it's none of your business who Ivy dates." She slid into the seat as Dean leaned in and kissed her on the cheek. Poppy looked at Ivy. "Are you sure you'll be okay?"

Ivy rolled her eyes. "Yes, now go. I'm freezing out here."

"I really wish you would reconsider. You shouldn't have to spend Christmas alone."

Poppy had invited her to spend Christmas in The Hamptons at Dean's summer vacation home, along with a few of his buddies from his law firm. *I would rather spend Christmas with a serial killer than have to spend one more minute with Dean.*

Her past three Christmas rituals were far better than staying in an oversized, overpriced five-bedroom beach house full of horny men reliving their fraternity years. No thanks! Staying home by herself, sitting on her black leather couch in front of the fireplace in her comfy p.j.s, slurping down a big bowl of Ramen Noodles sounded like heaven compared to the Christmas Frat House nightmare.

"Poppy, you worry too much. Besides I'm sure Mark," Ivy shot Dean a cross glare, "has something planned for us."

Poppy stuck out her bottom lip, giving her a pout that surely would work on Dean but not on her friend. "Go get warm. I'll see ya next year." Ivy waved goodbye as Dean rolled up the window and sped off.

Ivy closed the big glass door behind her and turned the lock. Her black heels echoed across the empty studio as she walked over to the displays to shut off the

3

spotlights. Indeed, it had been a successful night; four out of her five paintings had been bought at top dollar. But it was Poppy who had been the real star of the night; all of her showcased art had been purchased with inquiries on a few new projects. Who would have thought contemporary-western style wild animals in their natural states, add in one or two vibrant colors, would be such a winner? Ivy shook her head as she studied one of Poppy's paintings of a bear standing in a crisp stream with a flopping bright peach salmon in his mouth. She had a talent in capturing the animals' true essences.

Finally, Ivy reached the last painting. It was the only one of hers remaining that had not been purchased, and she was relieved to still have it. It was by far her favorite and most personal, because she had dreamt of such a place.

In the painting there were two Scottish Highland mountains peaked with white snow, a fine mist covered the sky and wisped over a winter garden, tingeing everything with grayness. A black iron gate, ajar, was covered in an array of green shades of ivy. Farther into the garden a bright green holly tree stood tall with ruby-red berries shining like stars. Fresh snow powdered the ground and the tops of the trees. Standing in awe, she ran her index finger across the holly and swore she could feel its sharp edges pricking her finger. The garden called to her from deep inside, somewhere soul deep. If there was one Christmas wish she could wish with all her heart, it would be to jump into this winter garden and stay forever.

Ivy took a step back and smiled. She knew exactly where to hang it back at the townhome she rented. If fact if it hadn't been snowing, she would carry it home with her tonight, since she lived just down the street. "This will look perfect in my living room above the fireplace." Ivy clicked off the light then checked the back door to make sure it was locked. Tomorrow she would have to come back and unlock the gallery for the movers. Poppy had promised their clients that the paintings would be delivered before Christmas.

After one last glance at the winter garden, Ivy slipped on her coat, wool cap, and grabbed her purse. Taking the keys out, she made her way to the front door. Locking it behind her, she nuzzled deep into her coat as she walked down Main Street against the snow flurries. Of all nights, why had she decided to walk to work on the coldest night of the year?

Quickly, Ivy hustled down the sidewalk, noticing all the shops had their closed until next year signs hanging in the storefront windows. This was one of the downfalls of living in a tourist community. Not only were tourists few and far between, but also most of the locals in Highland Falls were traveling, visiting family during the holiday season. There were a few locals who stayed behind and braved the cold; but for the most part, Highland Falls was a ghost town. For Ivy this time of year was a reminder of the Christmas Curse.

She passed a small girl holding her father's hand, walking down the sidewalk. The child was beaming from ear to ear, which made Ivy smile. She had a bounce in her step Ivy could relate to. Her mother had told her time and again she was daddy's little girl. Nothing could be truer; she'd loved her dad.

Her father Martin Davenport was an intelligent man, an Archaeologist specializing in the study of Celtic History. When he wasn't in Scotland on archaeological digs, which was rare, he spent his time teaching Medieval European History at NYU.

A memory, a special one that she had hung onto over the years crept into her thoughts and made her smile.

It was a few days before Christmas Eve and the night of the Winter Solstice. Her father had just returned home from a month's stay in Scotland where he had been head-deep into a dig where they believed they had stumbled upon sacred ground dating back to the Celts of old. Ivy remembered the dark circles under her father's eyes and how exhausted he had been, but he still found the energy to take his daughter out to find the perfect Christmas tree. She was ten and still innocent in the ways the world. She had believed her parents were happy in life and loved one another, which she'd found out mere hours ago was far from the truth. Earlier that day she'd heard her mother on the phone venting about how she was tired of coming in second place to Martin's work. That he lived and loved in the past.

But that night, surrounded by tall, full spruce trees, Ivy had been happy to have her father's undivided attention.

Ivy ran to her father, long blonde curls bouncing with every stride. "Dad," she pulled her father's arm excitedly, leading him over to a huge, green spruce, "Look! I found the biggest tree in the world!" She pointed.

"Yes, my love, you have." Martin chuckled as he glanced up and down, taking in the monstrous spruce.

"I want this one."

"I don't know, honey, it's very big. Do you think it will fit in the car?"

Ivy rolled her eyes. "Daaad, you put it on the roof of the car, not inside."

Her father pulled her wool cap down over her eyes. "Why of course, Ivy." He laughed and pulled his daughter close, hugging her.

They walked down another row of trees, holding hands. Ivy became quiet and withdrawn, deep in thought.

"What's wrong, Pumpkin?" Her father squeezed her close and kissed the top of her head.

Ivy kicked a clump of snow. "I miss you, Dad. Mom misses you too."

His forehead creased. "I know, but I'm home now."

"But for how long?"

"Ivy—"

"Dad, I heard Mom on the phone this afternoon. She sounded very upset with you. She said that she feels you love your work more than her."

Martin bent down to his daughter's level, holding her arms in his hands. "Pumpkin, you don't worry about me and your mother. I will take care of this. Understand me?"

"Yes, Dad." Ivy looked to the ground as a tear fell from her cheek.

"Did I ever tell you how your mother and I came up with your name?"

Ivy sniffled. "No."

"Come, walk with me."

They finished walking down the row of Christmas trees and stopped by a table that had all the trappings available to make your own holiday wreath. Martin grabbed a clump of holly and several vines of ivy. "There's an old legend about two Celtic Gods named Holly and Ivy who fell in love in a time where Gods were forbidden to."

"Ewww, Dad!"

He looked down at his daughter and grinned. "Holly was in great despair over this and he planted a holly tree in the enchanted garden for his love Ivy, so every time she passed the garden she would be reminded of Holly's love for her until they could be together again. Legend has it because of their loss and longing, the tree brings together others to help them find their true soulmates. When you *gather nine holly leaves," she watched her father grab nine holly leaves and stack them one on top of the other, "wrap a vine of ivy around the leaves like so, then place them under your pillow and make a wish, your wish will come true on the twelfth day of Christmas. But it only works for those pure of heart and who truly believe." He took the holly bundle and handed it to Ivy.*

Ivy flipped the bundle over and examined the leaves. "Dad, what does this have to do with me?"

Martin bent down and held her hand. "Your mom and I met under a holly tree and fell passionately in love. Every Christmas we went back to that tree, and just over ten years ago under that same tree, your mom told me she was pregnant with you. We decided to name you Ivy in honor of Ivy, the Celtic Goddess."

Ivy stood silent.

"So you see, Pumpkin, you have nothing to worry about. Your mom and I love each other very much."

Ivy wrapped her arms around her dad's neck and he squeezed her tight.

She wiped a tear from her cheek. She had believed in the old legend up until her father's death a year ago. Her wish never came true. Cancer took his life suddenly and her world fell apart.

Chapter Two

A few more blocks down Main Street and Ivy would be home, snuggling in the warmth of her house. The flurries were falling faster now and the bricked sidewalk was slippery with a thin layer of ice. With the thought of sipping hot cocoa and defrosting next to the fireplace, Ivy picked up the pace. She could smell that chocolatey goodness.

A buzzing sound coming from her purse interrupted her chocolate delight musings. She fumbled through her purse to find her cellphone. "Where is that damn thing?" Suddenly, her foot gave way from beneath her as she slipped on a patch of ice, twisting her ankle. She was about to hit the ground hard when strong arms gathered around her waist, pulling her against a solid wall of muscle, preventing her fall.

"That was a close one, lass. Are ye all right?" the stranger asked.

Ivy looked up at him and every coherent thought left her as she stared into the most intense dark eyes she had ever seen. It was as if those black depths held a spell and drew her in deep.

"Lass?"

Apparently she had stayed staring at him longer than she should. She couldn't tear her eyes away from his white t-shirt under his tan leather jacket, which fit him like a second skin, revealing he had muscles in all the right places. *He must think I'm an idiot.*

"Yes, I'm fine. Thank you." Embarrassed, Ivy tucked her hair behind her ears and pulled away from the stranger's arms, stumbling. She had an eerie feeling she'd felt his arms and his eyes on her before. But that was ridiculous!

Immediately, Ivy felt his strength again as he held her arm, helping her keep her balance. "I dinnae think ye're fine."

"I must have sprained my ankle." She bent down and removed her shoe. Already she could feel her ankle swelling.

"How far are ye walking? I can call ye a cab."

"Oh no, that's not necessary. I'll be fine. Really." Ivy began to take a step and buckled. Not happening. Her ankle was too painful to put pressure on it.

The stranger chuckled. "I understand that women value their independence, but, lass, ye won't make it another step without me help. Let me call for a cab."

"I only live two more houses down the street." Ivy pointed to the baby-blue, two-story wood frame townhome.

"All right." The stranger bent down and placed her arm around his shoulders. "Hang on, lass, I'll get ye home and off yer ankle in no time." He winked and it took all

11

of Ivy's will not to melt right there on the sidewalk. Thank God he was holding her, because her knees went weak.

Two stone accented townhouses later and there they stood outside her home. Awkwardly, they made it up three steps to her front door without any further embarrassment on Ivy's part. The heat she felt against his chest was instantly lost when the stranger took a step back, leaving her propped up next to the door.

"Do ye need help inside?"

Why yes she did. There was nothing more she wanted to do than invite him in and rip off his clothes and attack him like some wild, wanton woman. The man was intoxicating, making her want to throw caution to the wind, which was not like her in the slightest.

Ivy cleared her throat. "No, I can take it from here." She smiled meekly as she searched for the keys in her purse.

"Well then I bid ye a good night, Miss Davenport."

Ivy paused then looked up from her purse…the man was gone.

Wait…What? He knows my name?

She turned her head to the right then to the left, looking down the street, but there was no sign of him. It was as if he never existed. Poof…he was gone. And she hadn't even had a chance to thank him or ask his name. If her ankle wasn't swollen, she'd run after him.

Odd as it was, Ivy shook him from her thoughts and quickly unlocked the door. Before she entered the house she reached down and picked nine holly leaves from a holly bush she had planted next to the entrance years ago when she moved in.

It was reckless of her to allow a stranger to walk her home. Whoever this man was, he now knew where she lived. What if he came back? After the way he'd left, maybe he'd been stalking her all along. With a sense of dread creeping up her spine, Ivy limped into the house and locked both locks, then peeked out the living room window. Still, the man with strong hands and haunting eyes was nowhere to be seen.

A beep coming from her purse drew her attention to the fact that she had missed a call. *Shit!* It was probably Mark. With the phone in her hand, she slipped out of her coat and scrolled down to her missed calls. Yep, she was right; Mark had called. She'd missed him tonight at the gallery. She'd been hoping he would make it to the event. He'd told her if he could manage to leave work early, he would be there. Work ended at 6:30; the event had stared at 7. The signs of his undependability were already there, staring her in the face, even though they hadn't been dating long. No matter who the man was, it took time for Ivy to open up and allow herself to let her guard down. Too many times she'd been dumped and she had grown tired of the excuses. *You work too much. I don't feel a*

13

connection. It's not you, it's me, babe. I don't want to be tied down. Blah...Blah...Blah. She'd heard it all before.

This time she'd hoped Mark was the one. Someone to stand by her and not run ahead to a place where Ivy didn't feel comfortable going. Someone to support her and be a shoulder to cry on when life dealt her a bad hand.

Ivy held her cell to her ear and listened to the message. Mark's voice was clipped and cold as he told her he did not want to see her again. She sighed, frowning, her shoulders slumped as she plopped down heavily on the sofa. She'd been dumped by voicemail. Now that was a first. "Asshole!" She threw the messenger of bad news across the room. This was the third time in the last three years she had been through a breakup. Was she really that undateable?

Agreed, she did work a lot of hours and tended to immerse herself in her painting. Agreed, it took her more time than most women to trust the opposite sex. Agreed, in the last year she had gone through hell, tending to her father on his deathbed, watching the chemo drain every ounce of his once true self from his body, turning him into a feeble, sick man. And it had happened around Christmas. Ivy sat back against the couch and exhaled. There was no doubt the Christmas Curse was upon her.

Reaching into her coat pocket, she retrieved the holly leaves. Wincing, she stood and limped to the kitchen where her ivy plant sat on the breakfast bar. She snapped off a vine with three leaves on it and wrapped it around the holly, then placed it on the counter. "Stupid wives'-tale." She glared at the bundle.

Before she made an attempt to climb the stairs to her bedroom, she grabbed the pain relievers, an ice pack from the freezer for her swollen ankle, and a bottle of red wine to nurse her fragile ego back to health. The breakup wasn't what bothered her the most; it was the ugly pattern of things that concerned her. Perhaps she needed a change of scenery…a change of attitude. Or above all, better judgment when it came to dating men.

She turned and looked at the holly and ivy mocking her from the bar. Shaking her head, disgusted with herself because she was actually surrendering to the old Celtic folklore, she picked up the greenery and headed upstairs.

Dragging her swollen ankle behind her, she made it to her bedroom where she undressed and slipped into her nightgown. Limping into the bathroom, she brushed her teeth and washed the makeup off her face. Taking a moment, she glanced at her reflection in the mirror. Dark circles, bloodshot eyes. She rubbed her face. *Ivy, you look tired.* Indeed, she had been working too hard and needed a break.

She shut off the light and made her way to the bed. As she pulled the sheets back, the holly and ivy bunch fell to the floor. Gingerly, she bent down and picked it up. Holding the leaves in her hand, she closed her eyes and wished for once in her life that fate would listen to her pleas. She wanted her soul to be at peace.

Feeling silly for believing in such nonsense, Ivy nevertheless placed the bundle under her pillow, then took a sip from the wine bottle before crawling into bed. Her eyes were heavy, and before long, she found herself drifting off into a winter garden full of ivy and one giant holly tree. This is where she longed to be, for it called to her and settled her soul.

~~~~~

A cold breeze blew over Ivy's body, causing her to shiver as she reached for the big warm comforter. She reached farther and yet there was no comforter. She must have kicked it to the floor sometime during the night. She tucked her legs against her stomach to ward off the cold. Really she should get up and check the thermostat.

Ivy wrinkled her nose as the scent of pine and earth assaulted her. It smelled like…Christmas? Tree branches brushed together making an eerie sound. Had she left a widow open? She didn't remember opening one. How much wine had she drunk last night?

Her head pounded in pain and her thoughts spun as she tried to wake. It was so cold, almost as if she was outside. Ivy opened her eyes. A white haze blanketed everything in sight. Snow powdered the ground, the tops of trees, and collected on a wrought-iron fence surrounding her. She took in an enormous holly tree, following its thick trunk all the way to the top; pale green ivy intertwined through the holly's branches as if it was hugging the tree. Pushing herself up, she shook her head desperately, trying to make sense of it all.

Ivy stood weakly, shaking from the bitter cold. "This can't be," she whispered as she spun around in disbelief. "It's my winter garden." She felt a rush of elation that was immediately overshadowed by confusion and dread. Rigid with shock, she could not move or think. But she could not stand here until the snow and wind made her too weak to leave.

In a daze, Ivy opened the iron gate and stumbled outside, searching for something that felt familiar. The moon was big and bright in the sky, bright enough to shine through the grayness of the night. In the shadows, she could barely make out the massive snow-covered mountains standing in the distance and what looked to be a small town up ahead. There were no roads leading to it, no traffic sounds, and not one light was lit throughout. Blowing against the night chill, she saw smoke billow from the roofs of small huts peppered over the hillside. *Where I am?* she wondered. *And how did I get here?*

The wind howled and a gust of frigid air blew through her thin nightgown, stinging her skin. She wrapped her arms around her chest to protect herself against the cold, but Old Man Winter had already conquered her bones. Her body shivered and shook, beyond her control, and her teeth chattered violently. She was in desperate need of shelter before she fell victim to hypothermia.

17

Snow crunched beneath her numb bare feet as she made her way to the village. The trail was long, but fighting against the winter winds and bone-chilling cold weighed her down and drained her of energy, making the journey seem much longer than it was. Ivy prayed that this village wasn't a delusion, for she could feel her once sharp mind gradually becoming foggy. "Please…let there be shelter," she hissed against the snow flurries.

Weary, huddled over and rubbing her arms ineffectively to try to stay warm, she was frozen to the core when she reached town. No one was about. *Of course not,* Ivy mussed. *They are all inside sheltered from the bitter cold.* Her desire for warmth drove her farther as she came to a small hut. She knocked on the door. "Please, I need help," she called out, teeth chattering. "Please, I'm very cold."

Defeated, Ivy took a step back when no one came to the door. After a while when there was no response, she shoved the door open and was greatly relieved that no one met her with a weapon.

"Hello, is anyone here?" Her voice shook and traveled through the dark space. The hut smelled horrible, like horse shit, but she didn't care; it was warm inside. The moon shined through a small window and Ivy noticed a mound of hay in the corner. As though her body had taken over her logical thinking, she lay down and snuggled deep into the hay. Keeping sane was impossible when she was losing her mind little by little from the hypothermia. She could have sworn she heard a

18

horse whinny. Her mind drifted farther away from her until she lost consciousness and everything turned black.

Chapter Three

"Da!" The eldest MacLachan boy ran into his father's solar, out of breath. "Ye must come quick."

Kellen MacLachan drained his tankard of ale, caring not that the sun had barely risen. "Patrick," he wiped the amber liquid from his lips, "what has ye in such a panic this morn?"

Patrick pulled out the chair his father was sitting in and tugged at his arm. "Come, ye'll see."

Kellen stood on drunken legs. "If this be one of yer tricks, ye'd best no' let me catch ye."

"Nay, Da, no trick. I promise."

Slowly, Kellen lifted himself from the chair and grabbed the wooden staff that lay next to him, resting on his desk. Gaining his balance, which would have been much easier if he had stopped the ale two tankards ago, he followed his son out of the castle and toward his horse barn.

Patrick ran ahead, hardly waiting for his father. Kellen limped along, cursing every step of the way. A mere leg wound was not just cause for his commander to take him off the battlefield and send him home. He still had two arms that could masterfully wield a sword and bring down its wrath upon his enemy with great strength. The Highlander was a warrior; the heat of battle had been born in his veins and trained upon his body, passed down from his Irish kin. He was built for action.

Alas, the luck of the Irish hadn't shined upon his wife. On his return over a year ago, his world had changed, leaving him not only physically wounded but also emotionally destroyed. The announcement that his daughter had been born made his heart beat joyfully, until the room fell silent. His older brother Donnelly took over and walked with Kellen up the stairs to deliver the bad news; his wife had died during childbirth and left him and Donnelly to raise their three sons and his infant daughter alone. Indeed, a year had passed, but the wounds still ran deep and raw.

"Look, Da." Patrick pointed toward a heap of hay where his little brother Wylie was throwing oats at an unconscious woman lying on her back. Halting his oat assault, Wylie faced his father. "She will no' wake, Da."

"And she be wearing nothin' but her shift." Thaddeus, the middle child, ran by and slapped Wylie on the back of his head.

"I hate ye, ye turd!" Wylie yelled at his brother while chasing him through the barn and out the door.

Kellen stood over the woman and tapped her bare thigh with his walking cane. "Lass." He pushed farther with the cane and still the woman didn't move. Panic pricked through his drunken state, sobering him. There was a dead woman in his barn. *What in the devil has happened to her? How did she end up in my barn?*

21

"Patrick, go fetch a blanket. Quickly."

"Aye."

With much effort, Kellen bent down and leaned over her, trying to hear if she was breathing. He looked to her chest, catching a glimpse of the top of her naked breasts peeking out from under her nightgown. Shaking his thoughts away from her beauty, he saw her chest rise and fall. Thank God she was breathing.

Running back into the barn, Patrick handed a plaid to his father and bent over, clutching his hands to his thighs as he caught his breath. "Da, what are we going to do wit' her?"

Kellen tucked the plaid around the woman. Her skin was ice-cold and her lips were tinged blue. If this woman had a chance of surviving, he had to get her warm. There was no way he would allow her to die in his barn, or furthermore, on his property.

"What in the devil is this?" his brother Donnelly questioned as he strode next to Patrick, gawking at the woman.

Kellen stood and leaned on his cane. "I dinnae know, brother. I was hoping ye would." He pinned his brother with a scrutinizing glare.

"Och, ye dinnae think I did this?"

Kellen stood silent.

"I've never seen the lass before in me life, I assure ye."

"'Tis no matter. She's barely breathing and we need to get her warm before she dies."

"Aye." Donnelly bent down and scooped the woman into his arms. Listless, her body limply flopped against his chest and she began to mumble.

"Patrick, make sure there's a fire started in the hearth of me bedchamber," Kellen ordered.

"I'm taking her to yer bedchamber?" Donnelly asked with a bit of suspicion.

Kellen looked at the helpless woman in his brother's arms and nodded, confirming his mad request. Someone would be looking for her. She was someone's daughter or mayhap she had a husband out searching for her. The lass had to belong somewhere and before he was accused of a crime, he wanted to talk to the lass to find out what her story was. That is if she made it through the cold that plagued her body.

~~~~~

Kellen pulled the covers back from his bed while Donnelly lay the lass down.

"Her clothing is wet," Donnelly mentioned as he backed away from the bed. "We should remove it."

Kellen scrubbed a hand down his face. Already breaking his rule of never allowing a woman in his bedchamber, he now had to undress her in the sacred space that he had once shared with his wife.

"Ye're right, brother."

Donnelly moved toward the bed and pulled the furs back. Kellen grabbed his arm. "Nay, I'll do it. I found her on me land, she's me responsibility."

"Kellen, ye dinnae have to do this. I can take care of her."

The bond Donnelly had with his brother was strong, unbreakable, especially since his sister-in-law's death. He'd heard the screams through sleepless nights when Kellen had laid in bed for days on end, mourning his wife. With every tankard of ale he watched slip further into the darkness, until he was comfortably numb.

Shocked at how far Kellen had taken his madness, Donnelly had come home one eve to find all the female servants gone, except for the wet nurse. And if it wasn't for his daughter, she would have been gone as well. Females were not welcome at castle MacLachan and having a woman, soon to be naked, in his bed surely wasn't in Kellen's best interest.

"I know what ye be thinking, that I can no' handle it." And perhaps he couldn't, but somewhere deep within, Kellen was compelled to help the lass, as if he held the burden of her safety on his shoulders. Or mayhap he wanted to be there when she opened her eyes—to confirm they were just as stunning as her beauty.

24

Once Upon a Winter Solstice

Gently, the Highlander sat on the side of the bed and lifted her gown over her shaking thighs. Accidentally the back of his hand brushed against her skin. Her legs were long and slender, soft to the touch. As he pressed on, a small piece of black lace covering her womanly part peaked his interest. He'd never seen something so erotic on a woman before. Feeling guilty for staring too long, he looked over his shoulder and wasn't surprised to see Donnelly standing behind him, looking at the lass as if she was his prey.

"God's Blood, brother, show the lass some respect."

Feeling awkward, Donnelly cleared his throat, then turned his back.

Kellen continued to work the thin material up her body and paused as it reached her breasts. They were full, well-proportioned with the rest of her body, and he bet they felt as soft as they looked. Swallowing hard, he tamped down the urge to reach out and touch them.

"Are ye done?" His brother asked, shaking him from his lustful thoughts.

As much as her body enticed him, he hurried to remove the gown then tossed it to the ground. Grabbing the furs nearby, he tucked them around her, pushing away the images of her naked body and cursing himself for thinking upon her with such wicked thoughts.

"Aye." Kellen stood and took a step away from the lass.

She was still shivering uncontrollably. Kellen walked over to the hearth and threw another log on the fire. The flames hissed as they grew higher.

"What do we do now?" Donnelly inquired as he stood with his hands on his hips, looking at the lass.

Kellen stood and met his brother beside the bed. He'd tried everything to keep her warm, but it wasn't enough. A thought arose which confirmed he was losing all good sense, yet nothing felt more right. "She needs more warmth." Setting his cane next to a table by his bed, he removed his long furred jacket, then his tunic.

"What are ye doing?" Donnelly asked as if his brother had gone mad.

"'She needs our body heat." Kellen untied his trews and had begun to pull them down when his brother stopped him.

"Under no circumstances am I getting naked and lying in bed wit' yer ugly arse. Ye've gone daft. What happens when she wakes and finds yer ugly naked arse next to hers?"

"What will happen if she dies? How do we explain how we found her in me barn? Ye are aware how people judge first, then seek the truth."

In fact, Donnelly knew this all too well. He shook his head in surrender. "Bloody Hell." He kicked his boots off and undressed.

Once Upon a Winter Solstice

Kellen pressed his body against the lass and rubbed her shoulders and arms in hopes of giving her the warmth she needed. She was so cold. The bed gave way when Donnelly joined them. "Brother, ye're in debt to me until ye lay cold in the grave," he huffed as he settled behind the woman.

"We'll both be in the grave if the lass does no' wake."

A long silence crept over the room, leaving Kellen warring with himself as to whether he had made the right decision? Instinctively he brushed the lass's long blonde hair away from her face. Her nose was pert, slightly lifted. Giving in, he traced her round cheeks with the back of his hand, marveling in her beauty. He'd never seen a woman quite like her before.

His body stilled and his heart raced when the lass moved. This was what he feared the most, the woman waking naked in bed with two strangers. She nuzzled deep into his chest soft hot breaths heated his skin as she rested her head on his chest. He found himself wrapping his arms around her and pulling her close. Aye, he'd missed a woman's touch.

A sense of calm washed over him, a peace he hadn't felt in years. His eyes grew heavy and he fell asleep.

Chapter Four

Ivy plunged deeper into the warmth that surrounded her like a cocoon, yet she craved more. She inhaled, taking in a scent of pine mixed with something she couldn't put her finger on, but whatever it was, it was divine.

An image flashed before her; she was opening the iron gate to a winter garden; holly and ivy leaves glistened in the snow. Then the bite of winter stung straight to her bones, causing a shiver. The image felt dreamlike, yet as real as if she'd been there before.

Ivy opened her eyes, blinking away the fog. Wide-eyed, she was in shock and froze when a wall of hard, masculine muscle came into view. Slowly she glanced up, careful not to awake whoever was next to her, until she could see the man's face. Long, black lashes lay soft against his cheeks and his lips were partly open, snoring. *What the hell is going on?* She had a vague memory of another strange, uncomfortable occurrence, but she could not make it come into focus. All she knew was that everything was wrong.

Trying not to panic, Ivy lifted the furs and peeked underneath, then slowly scooted away from the man. They were both naked. How did this happen? Had someone drugged her?

Once Upon a Winter Solstice

Ivy froze when a tree branch of an arm swung around and landed across her waist. She closed her eyes and held her breath; she was pinned between two men with nowhere to go. What was she going to do? She had no idea where she was, and by judging the size of these two men, she had no chance of escaping.

At that moment the man behind her rolled over on his side and pulled her close. Ivy tamped down a scream that climbed her throat as she felt his cock brush against her backside. That was it. It was either fight or die trying.

In one fluid motion Ivy shoved her feet forward, connecting with the man's stomach in front of her while at the same time throwing her head back and slamming it straight into the man's nose behind her. In an instant both men awoke shouting in pain, rolling off the bed. Quickly Ivy looked around the room for a weapon. Grabbing the walking cane, she scooted to the head of the bed and gathered the furs around her. "Who are you and where am I?"

Doubled over, holding his stomach, Kellen howled in pain. "Bloody Hell, woman!"

"Are ye daft?" Donnelly held his nose as blood trickled down his lip. "This is the gratitude I get for helping save yer life? Kellen, the wench is yer problem now." Donnelly grabbed his trews and strode out of the bedchamber.

Tucking the fur around her, Ivy stood on the bed holding the cane like a Samurai warrior. "I said who are you?"

"I would like to know the same aboot ye." With haste, Kellen pulled up his trews and tied them.

"What do you mean? You brought me here."

"Nay, lass, my son found ye in me barn, unconscious and aboot to meet yer death. I want to know why ye are here."

That was exactly what she wanted to know. Taken aback, Ivy remembered the garden as it slowly came into focus, but she had no recollection of a barn.

"Are ye a spy?"

Ivy cocked her head to the side. "Spy?"

"Aye. I have no' seen ye before on me land." Kellen took a step forward and Ivy shoved the cane toward him, warning him to stay away.

"I am no spy."

"Then who are ye?"

Ivy observed the man as he pulled a tunic over his head and adjusted it. She looked the room over in hopes of finding some kind of familiarity. The fireplace that took up half a wall roared with flames, heating and lighting the space. Furs covered the bed and colorful tapestries hung on the walls. Ivy's heart raced when she

30

saw the stone walls. Had she been kidnapped and held in a dungeon? Oh, God, what kind of trouble was she in? *Where* am *I? And how did I get here? It seems impossible. It makes no sense!*

"Where am I?" Ivy asked, hoping her voice hadn't given away how scared she was.

"Castle MacLachan of the Black Hills," he replied.

"And who are you?"

"Me name is Laird Kellen MacLachan of Clan MacLachan and this is me home."

Ivy listened intently to the man's voice. His accent was thick and at times hard to understand, but she'd learned enough from her father to know it was most definitely Scottish or Irish. His clothing was very old-fashioned, and if she had to guess—again, based on what she had learned from her father—dated back to medieval times. His hair was dark and hung past his broad shoulders. She noticed a limp as the man came closer to the bed, and she followed him with her eyes.

"I mean ye no harm, lass. I just need to know who ye are and why ye are here. I'm sure someone is out looking for ye."

Ivy relaxed a bit, knowing she hadn't been brought here with ill intensions, yet she still didn't trust him or this place. Her head throbbed and her thoughts spun out of control as she dropped to her knees. He wrapped his

31

strong arms wrapped around her, catching her before she fell off the bed.

"Please," she said weakly, "don't hurt me."

"Lass, ye're under me protection. No harm will come to ye. I swear me life on it."

The man lifted her legs and tucked her back in bed. "Ye're still verra weak from the cold. I'll have some hot broth brought up to ye. Rest and we'll talk later."

The last thing she remembered before she fell asleep was his soft comforting touch, brushing her hair away from her face.

~~~~~

Ivy woke to a rustling sound. Startled, she sat up to find a young woman in the room searching for something in the dark wardrobe.

"What are you doing?"

Startled, the young woman turned around. "Pardon me, mistress. The laird has asked me to see to yer every need. There's broth on the table and I'll have a dress for ye soon." She smiled and turned back to the wardrobe.

On guard, Ivy wrapped a fur around her body and got out of bed, eyeing the vaulted ceiling stained by soot, the walls made of rough-hewn stone, the faded rug on the floor, the carved table on which a steaming bowl sat with some flat bread. Her stomach growled as she sat down and blew on a spoonful of broth. The aroma was pleasant, although the presentation of the food was less appealing. She ate it anyway. "What's your name?" she asked, wiping the corner of her mouth.

"Me name is Moina." The girl went to straighten the covers on the bed.

Ivy sat and watched her. She looked young, perhaps eighteen. Her black hair was braided high on her head.

"Do you work here for…the laird?"

"Aye, I be a wet nurse for his daughter."

"A wet nurse?" Ivy thought that odd; wet nurses didn't exist in the twenty-first century.

"Aye, me daughter and wee Breann are the same age. The laird has been verra good to me." Nervously, Moina laid a green gown on the bed, then stood with her hands folded in front of her, waiting for Ivy as she finished her broth.

Ivy eyed the girl, wondering why she hadn't left the room. "You don't have to stay and keep me company. I'll be fine."

"Mistress, I'm to stay here and assist ye with yer dress. The laird is waiting for ye in his solar. Ye can no' go to him wearing nothin' but yer skin."

A chill snaked up her spine and she pulled the fur tight around her shoulders as several impressions came together. The laird in his solar. The ancient feel of this room, the clothing the two strange men had worn.

33

Everything was odd here. Wrong. Out of place. The scenery was different, the accents and language were different, the whole vibe since she'd awakened was different. She furrowed her brow and thought back to the stories her father had told her about ancient times— about the Celts and the way they'd lived. It struck her then with the force of a devastating blow. She was no longer in the twenty-first century; she was in medieval Scotland. Her vision blurred and she found she could not breathe.

~~~~~

Kellen sat behind his large desk signing the two charters that had been awaiting his attention for at least a fortnight. Today he had changed his routine, surprising even his brother. A few hours ago at the morning meal, he'd exchanged the ale he usually consumed with extra blood pudding, then hurried to his solar where business was stacked deep. He couldn't quite explain what compelled him to want to start the day sober, but that urge drove him to try to be the laird his father would have been proud of. The laird he had once been.

"Brother, do ye think the lass could be a spy?" Donnelly asked.

"I do no' know. 'Tis me hope that she will tell us everything we need to understand her situation." Kellen signed a parchment, then set it aside.

"And if she refuses?"

Kellen rubbed the back of his neck. "She'll stay here until she talks or until someone claims her."

"Do ye think that's a good idea? There hasn't been a female allowed within these walls in over a year."

"Moina is still here."

Donnelly paused. "That's different. She's needed."

"Breann is auld enough now for Patrick to take care of. Mayhap 'tis time for Moina to go back home."

"*This* is Moina's home," Donnelly bit back. "Besides yer boys are heathens. Mayhap 'tis time ye buried the ghost and found a wife."

Kellen fell silent and pinned his brother with a harsh glare. His jaw ticked at Donnelly's verbal kick in the ballocks.

A tap on the door grabbed his attention. "Enter," Kellen called out.

Moina entered the room along with Ivy.

His breath hitched in his lungs. The woman was stunning. Even though he had liked her long blonde hair hanging freely, now, with the stands woven in a thick braid, he could see her full beauty. Her face was flawless; her jawline was strong, yet feminine, and her neck was made for kisses.

With respect, Moina curtsied and elbowed Ivy in the ribs when she didn't follow suit. Quickly, Ivy curtsied.

35

Kellen stood and walked around to the front of his desk, leaning against it with his arms crossed over his chest. "How do ye fare, lass?" he asked the woman.

"I'm well."

"Good, I'm hoping ye're ready to tell me who ye are and why ye were in my barn, naked."

Ivy lifted her chin. "I'm not telling you anything until you tell me why I was in bed with two naked strangers."

"Woman, watch yer tongue. Ye be speaking to Laird MacLachan son of O'Neil and great-grandson of the Irish prince, Prince Anrothan. Ye'd be wise to address the laird properly," Donnelly demanded.

"Well, please pardon my informality," she said sarcastically.

Kellen stood back, intrigued by the woman's boldness. She wasn't like Moina, meek and obedient. In fact, the woman was enticing as she stood pouting. Aye, there was something pleasantly alluring about her.

"As I said, my son found ye in me barn, cold and unconscious. My brother and I brought ye into our home to make sure ye stayed warm and survived through the night. We meant ye no harm. We were gentlemen, I can assure ye."

"Thank you. I wish I could remember how I got here."

Kellen's brows furrowed. "Lass, ye remember nothin'? No' even yer name?"

"No, my name is Ivy Davenport."

"Where are ye from, Ivy Davenport? I'm sure ye have a husband oot searching for ye."

"No, I'm not married and I'm sure your wife would not be pleased to know you were in bed naked with another woman.

"Me wife has been dead for a year now." For the first time since she had passed, he'd said those words out loud. Before, emotions had run too deep for him to accept that she was gone. Furthermore, he'd spent the last year in a drunken mind-numbing state. Drinking ale quieted his demons.

Ivy's mood softened a bit. "I'm so sorry."

Aye, the lass was hiding something. She was skirting around his question. The way she talked and her demeanor were like nothing he'd seen before. Kellen paused as he thought about choosing his next words properly. Donnelly was right; his children were running amok and he hadn't been much help in disciplining them. Mayhap his brother was right, it was time to give up the ghost.

"Och, lass, it has been brought to me attention that I could use a woman around here," Kellen shot Donnelly a stern glare. "And since ye will no' tell me where ye've come from, ye'll stay here until we solve this mystery."

"No. you can't keep me here against my will. Someone is out looking for me. So, I thank you for your hospitality, but I must be leaving." Ivy said the only words she could think of, because she knew no one was searching for her. She didn't understand what had brought her to this medieval castle and these strangers she had never imagined. All she knew was that she wanted to go home. Turning around, she headed toward the door.

Donnelly stood, blocking it, with his arms folded across his chest. Ivy paused then faced Kellen. "You told me you weren't going to harm me."

"Och, lass, I'm a man of me word. Ye're under me protection."

"Then why can't I leave? I want to go home."

Kellen walked toward Ivy; their gazes locked. "Ye haven't told me where home is. I would be breaking my oath to protect ye if I let ye go, no' knowing where ye're going."

Ivy swallowed hard and began to heat under his smoldering stare.

"Besides," he bent his head so his lips brushed her ear, "I'm no' ready to let ye go."

Kellen walked past her, making his way to the door. He stopped short and addressed his brother. "See to it that Moina shows our guest what is expected of her."

Chapter Five

The day had been long and brutally rough for Ivy. Before she could finish one task, Moina was barking out orders to start another. The stone floors in the great hall had been swept, the bedchambers had been tidied, and there Ivy had the pleasure of experiencing firsthand the cleaning of chamber pots. She'd even swept the hearths of ash and stacked a supply of wood in each room so that every bedchamber would have plenty to keep a warm fire through the night. She had never expected to find herself in a castle, but she was learning all about this one in the worst way possible.

Ivy had a strange feeling that Moina was taking a bit of jealousy out on her, working her extra hard so she would fail. Ivy tried to make small-talk, to learn more about the laird and his family, but it was like talking to the wall. A nod was the best response she had received.

She couldn't blame the girl for being jealous, even though she was angry at him for not letting her leave, there was no escaping the fact that Kellen MacLachan was handsome, and once pinned with that smoldering gaze of his, any woman would go up in flames—even a woman from the twenty-first century.

Furthermore, from what Moina had told her she'd been a huge influence in raising his daughter. It was obvious Moina was in love with Laird MacLachan, and with no other women in the castle that she'd noticed, Ivy realized she was a threat.

Ivy left the last bedchamber and made her way downstairs to the next chore—the kitchen. As she did, she took in more of the castle. Her father would have been in heaven here. The architecture alone would have fascinated him. She envisioned her dad studying the stone walls, feeling their rough textures and wondering how they completed such a massive structure without modern technology. And here she was experiencing actual medieval life. How could that be?

Of course Moina gave her vague directions to the kitchen; Ivy expected no less. She paused in a large open room filled with long plank tables and a large hearth, which took up much of the space on one wall. Remembering a picture of the inside of a castle that her father had taken on one of his research excursions to Scotland, she believed she was in the great hall, which meant the kitchen shouldn't be too far away.

She walked across the hall and rounded the corner to find the kitchen. Moina was bustling around, making up for lost time. "Ivy, where have ye been? We have to prepare for tonight's feast."

"A feast?"

"Aye, a feast," Moina said irately. "Every Winter Solstice we celebrate light and rebirth. A new beginning."

Ivy paused, trying to put the pieces together about this place. From what she recalled, it was believed Druid Pagans celebrated the Winter Solstice as their way of honoring light in a time where the days grew darker. It was a time of rebirth, a time in which the festivities never stopped. This led her to believe Christmas was not a tradition here as a way to celebrate Christ's birth.

At that moment Donnelly and Kellen entered the kitchen. Donnelly with a huge, dead boar wrapped around his shoulders.

"I see the hunt went well, me laird," Moina said, turning her once sour attitude to nice and sweet.

"Aye," Kellen replied as Donnelly slammed the young boar on the table in front of Ivy.

"We were lucky to catch the bastard. It gave a good chase," Donnelly added.

"We shall have a big feast tonight," Kellen said, then stabbed the wooden table with a knife.

In shock, Ivy looked at the dead animal, then at Kellen. "And what do you expect me to do with it?" She nodded to the boar.

Kellen reached over the table and wiped a smear of black soot from Ivy's cheek. "We kill it, ye cook it." He smirked.

41

Telling herself not to look into his smoldering dark depths, she took a step back. "You are telling me that I have to skin this animal?"

"Aye," Kellen said confidently as he grabbed a handful of hazelnuts and popped one in his mouth.

"What's wrong, lass, dinnae ye eat where ye come from?" Donnelly asked.

"Of course I do. I just don't prepare it the way you do."

"Do the best ye can, lass. Ye're in good hands." Kellen smiled at Moina then quit the kitchen with Donnelly.

As the men left, in rushed Thaddeus and Wylie with a shield in one hand and a wooden sword in the other, pretending to fight to the death. Wood clashed together and echoed through the kitchen.

"Surrender, turd, and I'll show ye mercy," the youngest boy, Wylie shouted out.

"Ha-ha, never," Thaddeus boasted as he slammed his sword down and cracked Wylie's shield. "Ye fight like a girl."

They fought back and forth and ran around Ivy and the table where the boar lay. "The wench must die!" Thaddeus commanded.

Ivy's head was spinning from the noise and her stomach lurched as she grimaced at the boar. She was tired and was still feeling the effects of the cold. Moina did nothing to stop the boys or at least shoo them away from the kitchen. It was the last straw that broke her when Thaddeus poked her behind with his sword and declared, "Victory is mine!"

Ivy inhaled but it did no good, the last thread of sanity she had clung to frayed, and she exploded. "I've had enough, boys!" She grabbed a wooded spoon and began to chase them.

"What are ye doing? Have ye gone mad? These are the laird's boys," Moina shouted in disbelief.

"I don't care whose children they are, they need manners." Ivy reached out and missed snatching Wylie by the tunic by an inch. The boys banded together and ran out the back door of the kitchen. Ivy stopped short as she reached the threshold. "I know where you live!" she shouted after them. "You'll come back soon and I'll be waiting for you."

In retaliation, the boys stuck their tongues out and made rude faces.

"Brats," Ivy said under her breath as she turned to Moina, who was looking at her like she had gone completely insane. "And as for you," she stalked Moina, causing her to step back, "If you think for one minute I'm skinning that beast, you are terribly mistaken."

"Nay, I will do it." Moina strode to the table and busied herself in preparing the boar.

43

Ivy stood with her hands on her hips, trying to calm herself. As Moina sliced into the boar's flesh, Ivy wrinkled her nose and became nauseous at the sight.

"Ye dinnae look so good," Moina said. "Why dinnae ye go and fetch me some leeks and onions for this beast."

"Yes, I think I will. Anything is better than watching you hack away at that poor animal."

Moina pointed to the door. "The spence is right outside the kitchen and to your right."

Before Ivy stepped outside into the bitter cold, she grabbed a cloak hanging next to the door, wrapping the wool tightly around her shoulders.

Reaching the spence—or what she hoped was the spence—she slid the wooden latch over and opened the door to a cool and clean space. A few wooden tables sat along the walls, scattered with various sizes of bowls and jars but no vegetables. She walked deeper into the room, and in the corner was another small table with leeks and onions lying on top. Taking a basket hanging above the table, she started to fill it when the door slammed shut and the latch slid across the door. Giggles rang out from the other side of the door.

"No, no, no." Ivy ran to the door and tried to push it open, but it wouldn't budge. "Let me out, boys! Now!" She smacked the door. "Please!"

Her heart dropped when she heard the snow crunch as the boys ran off.

Once Upon a Winter Solstice

With her back to the door, Ivy slid down and pulled the cloak tighter around her body. How in the hell was she going to get out of here? She looked around the dark room, realizing there were no windows. She was living in hell; the Christmas Curse had followed her all the way to medieval Scotland.

~~~~~

Kellen was the last to join in the feasting as townsfolk and kin gathered in his great hall. He sat down across from Donnelly and his eldest son, Patrick. Thaddeus and Wylie sat next to each other giggling like little girls while Moina sat at the end, holding Breann.

"Moina, the boar is cooked to perfection," Donnelly said as he tore into its flesh.

With a beaming grin on her face, Moina smiled at him. "Thank ye."

"Aye, 'tis lovely," Kellen said as he watched his two sons whispering to each other, which he knew meant they were up to no good.

"Will Ivy be joining us this eve?" Kellen asked.

"My laird, I haven't seen Ivy since I asked her to go to the spence and retrieve some vegetables. She was rather ill upon the sight of me butchering the boar. She's probably resting. Shall I send Patrick to fetch her?"

At that moment Thaddeus and Wylie burst out in laughter.

"What is so funny, lads?" their father queried with a cross glare.

"Thaddeus made me do it, Da," Wylie confessed.

"Shut yer gob, turd." Thaddeus shoved his brother with his elbow and nearly knocked him off the bench.

"Boys." Kellen's voice boomed over the hall. "I want to know where Mistress Ivy is? What have ye done wit' her?"

Wylie stood and ran toward the kitchen before Thaddeus could catch him. "Da, I know, I know."

Kellen and Patrick rose, then took off after the boys. They followed them through the kitchen and out the back door to the spence, where Wylie was slapping at his brother to leave him alone. "She's in there, Da." The boy pointed to the door.

Quickly, Kellen opened the door and Ivy flew out of the room, nearly knocking Kellen down. "I told you I would get you." Madder than a wet hen, Ivy chased the boys. She chased them through the heavy snow until she lost her breath. She bent over to catch her breath and from out of nowhere a snowball hit her in the face. She shook off the white powder, then reached down with a devilish grin and scooped up a handful of snow, making it into a perfect tight ball. She straightened and threw the snowball, nailing Thaddeus in the head. "Take that, you brat!"

Once Upon a Winter Solstice

From behind she felt another snow-filled assault hit her back. In one fluid motion, she grabbed another handful of powder and swung around, hitting Wylie in the face. The battle of the snow continued until Kellen and Patrick reached the battlefield. "Enough!" Kellen's voice thundered.

In the heat of the moment Ivy whirled around and threw a snowball at Kellen, hitting him in the chest.

Everyone fell silent and stared at the laird. In shock, the boys stood with their mouths open, ready to feel their father's wrath.

Kellen shook like a wet dog while Ivy held her hand across her mouth to tamp down a laugh. Her eyes grew large when Kellen slowly bent down and gathered a fistful of snow. Ivy shook her head but it was of no use. A huge snowball flew across the distance between them and landed in her face. Now the real battle began. Snowballs of every size flew and connected with their targets. Thaddeus and Wylie joined Ivy as they ganged up against Kellen and Patrick. The battle was relentless.

Shielding himself from the attack, Kellen left his safe position and advanced on Ivy. Before she could run, Kellen grabbed her around the waist and they fell into the powdery snow, laughing.

Bracing himself, he rested his weight on his elbows, careful not to crush her. They locked eyes and the laughter stopped. He brushed a strand of blonde hair from her face. "Ye're verra beautiful when ye smile." He lowered his head, his lips brushing hers, and was pleasantly surprised when she didn't stop him. Ivy opened her mouth, inviting him in. He swept his tongue inside and deepened the kiss. His cock hardened when she threaded her fingers through his long dark hair. God's teeth, she tasted sweeter than honey.

A blast of cold snow hit their faces and broke the kiss. Kellen and Ivy looked up to find Patrick, Thaddeus, and Wylie standing above them with their arms crossed over their chests.

"Ewww!" Wylie exclaimed. "Kissy, kissy ewww la, la," he sang and shook his rear end back and forth.

Kellen threw a handful of snow at the boys and they ran off. He smiled down at Ivy. "I'm sorry. Me boys are heathens. Let's get ye inside and warm."

Chapter Six

Once inside the castle, Ivy helped Wylie out of his wet jacket and tunic while the other two children stripped out of their wet clothing. Kellen appeared with dry tunics and blankets. After the boys dressed, Kellen told his sons to go get warm by the fire.

Ivy finished wrapping a blanket around Wylie's shoulders, then tousled his dark hair. "You heard your father, now go…scram." She playfully smiled at the boy.

Kellen pulled off his tunic and Ivy went weak in the knees. She raked her eyes down his chest of well-defined sinewy muscle. Soft, brown hair lightly feathered his pectorals, his nipples were erect and dark and his skin prickled from the cold. She followed the brown trail of hair further until it stopped below his low-hanging trews. Her heart thumped against her ribcage as she fought to keep her balance.

"Ye should get oot of those wet clothes before ye catch yer death, lass," Kellen insisted as he bent down, removing his boots.

The word 'lass' rolled off his tongue in such a way that it left her body wanton and her thoughts growing wickedly out of control. She couldn't deny there was an instant attraction, which she had never before allowed herself to experienced. Her track record with men had been batting zero for the home team for as long as she could remember, so building a protective cocoon around her heart was the best way to protect herself and continue with the dating game.

But this man was different.

Kellen cleared his throat, bringing Ivy's attention back to the here and now. Shit, she had stared too long.

Before she knew what was happening, Kellen turned her around and unlaced the back of her dress, one tantalizing lace at a time. The dress began to fall and she clenched the wet material to her chest. She looked over her shoulder to find his hot gaze gliding over her bare skin. When their eyes met, he turned her around and unclenched her hand; the dress fell to floor.

Kellen readjusted the neckline of her dry shift so it was sitting on her shoulders, then he wrapped a blanket around her. "Ye should go get warm by the fire."

Ivy didn't know what to do or say. She wasn't used to someone taking care of her. She was an independent woman who took care of herself. And now she was allowing a man to take care of her, not once but twice. And it felt good.

Ivy nodded to Kellen then made her way to the hearth where Thaddeus and Wylie were sitting on a fur rug eating an oatcake while Patrick held his baby sister, singing to her. It was an odd sight at first after what she had just experienced with the boys. She stood back and took in the scene.

"These are me children." Kellen came over to her and stood, handing her an oatcake. "This is Patrick, my eldest."

Shyly, Patrick nodded his head.

"He's the one who found ye in me barn."

Wide-eyed from embarrassment, Ivy choked on a piece of the oatcake.

"Are ye alright, lass?"

Clearing her throat, Ivy nodded. "Yes."

"Ye've already met Wylie, me youngest, and Thaddeus, me pain in the arse," he said with a smile.

"I'm sure he's the spitting image of his father," Ivy teased.

"Och, I suppose some would say."

"And this here is me wee Breann." Kellen picked up his daughter from Patrick.

Ivy leaned toward Kellen to get a better view. "She's very pretty."

"Aye, Just like her mother." Kellen said as he tickled her tummy.

"She must have been a fine woman."

He handed Breann back to Patrick. "Aye."

51

Kellen went over to a table by the hearth and picked up a pitcher of ale. The itch was still there. "I came home from battle, wounded, to discover she had no' made it through the birth. I was devastated. She was a wonderful woman. As ye can tell by me children's lack of manners, my wife held our family together."

Ivy followed him to the table.

"I spent most of me time in battle when I should have been here. She deserved a better husband. And now me children deserve a better father." Kellen lifted the tankard to his lips when he was suddenly stopped.

Ivy took the tankard from his hand. "Everyone makes mistakes, and we have every right to redeem ourselves. Your wife was proud of you; I see that in your children. Your family has had to deal with a difficult loss. No one can fault you for that."

Kellen cupped her face and they locked eyes. "Where did ye come from?" he whispered then leaned in and kissed her lips.

God, the man felt so good. He kissed her with a passion that said she was the air he breathed. There was something else sitting deep within her core that was more than lust. There was a familiarity about him, a comfort, as if she had met him before, which was impossible. How could she have had met someone this far in the past? It wasn't possible, yet her heart told her differently.

Ivy stepped back from their embrace, breaking the kiss. "Kellen." She paused, uncomfortable and unfamiliar with the formalities. "I mean, my lord."

"Ye can call me Kellen." He pulled her back into his embrace and rested his forehead against hers.

Ivy closed her eyes, trying to fight the temptation to stay. "I should go," she whispered.

"If that is what ye wish." He kissed the tip of her nose. "Or ye could stay a wee bit longer." He wiggled his brows.

Ivy laughed. "Moina was relentless today. I'm exhausted."

"I'll talk to Moina aboot that. In the meantime, ye can take me bedchamber. I'll sleep in the boy's chamber tonight."

"Thank you." Ivy turned to leave and Kellen grabbed her arm. She caught his smoldering gaze. "Sleep well, Ivy Davenport." His voice was low and vibrated through her, and when he grinned, a dimple flashed through a shadow of whiskers, imprinting an image of pure maleness that Ivy wouldn't be able to erase from her mind. Sleep? She wouldn't be sleeping tonight.

Chapter Seven

Kellen woke with determination. Today he was going to find out who Ivy was and where she came from. The lass had swept into his life like a gust of wind, blowing it out of control in a very short amount of time.

He hadn't realized until last night how much he needed to hear those words that he wasn't past redemption. That he had time to redeem himself and become the father his children needed him to be. If fact, he had already taken the first step. He turned the ale away, thanks to a beautiful blonde-haired, blue-eyed lass.

If he was a man who believed in witchcraft, he would have thought himself bewitched by her. Nay, there was something more than witchery here.

Kellen opened the door to his bedchamber in search of a clue that Ivy might have left behind. He walked to the foot of the bed and picked up the nightgown she had been wearing the day Patrick found her in the barn. Kellen shook the soft material free then brought it to his nose. Closing his eyes, he inhaled deeply. *She smells sweeter than honey.*

As he went to lay the gown back on the bed, black lace material fell to the ground. He bent down and picked it up. A vision flashed and he recalled Ivy wearing the black lace under her nightgown. He examined it, rubbing the material in his hands. He'd never seen something so erotic before. *There's barely enough fabric here to cover her arse.*

"Kellen?" He heard Donnelly calling for him outside his bedchamber.

"Aye," Kellen replied and quickly hid the erotic black lace down his pants.

"I was hoping ye were in here. Yer door was left open."

"Och, Donnelly, I have to find oot where Ivy is from. The lass is a complete mystery to me. I've never felt so—"

"Completely overtaken by a lass?"

"Aye." Kellen walked the room from wall-to-wall in hopes of something grabbing his attention and satisfying his curiosity. But what was he looking for?

"Kellen, where is your cane?" Donnelly furrowed his brows.

His brother stopped in mid-stride as if it had just dawned on him. He looked at Donnelly. "I haven't needed the blasted piece of wood since I stopped drinking the ale."

Donnelly smiled. "I've seen a great change in ye, me brother, since Ivy has arrived."

"Aye. If I didn't know any better, I would think she's heaven sent. An angel."

Kellen heard a crunch beneath his boot. Bending down, he picked up a stack of holly leaves wrapped in ivy. "God's wounds." Kellen studied the winter greenery.

"What is it?" Donnelly asked, standing beside his brother.

Kellen handed him the bundle. "Are ye thinking what I'm thinking?"

Donnelly stood speechless as he stared at the holly and ivy. "It can no' be."

"The proof is right here. This explains everything, Donnelly. The legend is true. Holly and Ivy have sent me me true love."

"Aye, they have sent ye yer angel."

"What are you two doing in here?" Ivy stood outside the doorway with her hands on her hips.

Like a deer looking into a hunter's eyes, the brothers stood silent.

"I asked ye a question, my lord."

Ivy sounded too formal for his liking. "I told ye to call me Kellen. Donnelly was being an arse, threatening ye wit' formalities yesterday. He's still mad aboot ye breaking his nose."

"Ivy's hand flew over her mouth. "I broke yer nose?"

Donnelly glared at Kellen. "Ye didnae break it. Just a wee flesh wound."

"I'm so sorry. I—"

"Ye were protecting yerself. There's no need to be sorry." Kellen hoped that the diversion would make Ivy forget about her question, because he had no idea what to say, nor did he want to tell her about what he'd just found, not yet. "Och, Donnelly and I are going hunting, so I stopped by me bedchamber to grab me bow. We'll be going now." Kellen and Donnelly strode to the door.

"You mean that bow hanging on the wall?" Ivy pointed at the bow with suspicion.

Both brothers came to an abrupt stop. They had been found out.

"Ivy," Kellen turned and faced her, "this is me bedchamber and I can come and go as I please."

Ivy cleared her throat. "I asked you a question."

He ran his hand through his dark hair. "Lass, I've been patient wit' ye, but ye need to tell me right now where ye come from."

She hung her head and sighed in defeat. It was ridiculous. They would never believe her. Just as she would never believe such a tale if someone told it to her. But she had to try. She did not know what else to do. "I suppose you do need to know. It's only fair. But you'll doubt me, both of you. You must know that everything I'm about to tell you is the truth. I have no rhyme or reason to lie to you, Kellen."

"I understand." He crossed his arms.

~~~~~

Ivy didn't know where to start, for there was no easy way to say she was from the future without sounding mentally unstable. Could she trust that Kellen would believe her and help her find her way back to the winter garden in hopes of returning home, or would it be too much for him to grasp, so she would end up burning at the stake for witchcraft? Ivy sat heavily on the bed. She had to tell him everything and hope for the best if she had any chance of returning home.

"Kellen, Donnelly, I'm from the future, the twenty-first century. A time so different from yours that I cannot even begin to describe it so you would understand." Ivy paused, waiting for a response and when there was nothing but silence and slightly widened eyes, she continued. "I don't understand it myself. All I know is that before I went to sleep, I wished upon nine holly leaves wrapped in ivy, then I awoke in a winter garden, cold and in shock."

Donnelly turned abruptly. A soft whispered "shite" traveled through the room as he strode out of the bedchamber.

Ivy watched him leave, her heart thumping against her ribcage. She began to sweat. She prayed that she was doing the right thing, but she couldn't shake the haunting feeling that she was digging her own grave.

"Dinnae fash yerself over Donnelly." Kellen had to fight to get the words past his lips, but he was not certain if was out of fear or excitement. "Go on."

Inhaling, Ivy straightened her spine. "When I came to, my mind was spinning and I was freezing, so I started to search for shelter. I don't remember much about how I got to your barn. I'm guessing I became delusional from the hypothermia. I thought I was going to die."

"Hypothermia?"

"It's when you become extremely cold and you cannot retain your body's core temperature."

"Aye." He answered as if he understood, but Ivy knew better; he was confused.

"I don't know how I got here. As you can plainly see, I don't belong here."

"I agree. Ye are like no other I have ever met." Kellen sat down on the bed beside her.

"I need to go back to the garden. In hope I can find a way back home." Tears began to stream down her cheeks. "I just want to go home."

Kellen pulled her into his arms and held her as she broke down. "We'll find a way, lass."

Ivy sat up and wiped a tear away. "Then ye believe me?"

Warm hands cupped her face as he met her gaze. "'Tis a strange tale indeed, but somewhere deep inside, I do."

Ivy smiled, relieved that she wasn't going to burn.

"Ivy, I believe fate has brought ye here to me. Ye have made me desire to be a better man. As much as I want ye to stay, I will help ye find the garden on one condition."

Ivy slipped from his embrace, worried about his stipulation. "And what might that be?"

"Give me eight days to make ye fall in love wit' me." He leaned in and nuzzled her neck.

She closed her eyes and took him in. He had no idea how cursed she was when it came to love, but she wouldn't stop him from trying to break the Christmas Curse. If she believed, which she didn't, she had eight days until her wish was supposed to come true. She hesitated for only a moment, then nodded. She could give him the eight days.

"What if I don't fall in love with you?"

"Then I'll return ye to yer garden."

Ivy paused. A sneaking suspicion crept up her spine. "Kellen, do ye know about the Winter Garden Legend?"

He kissed her lips then stood. "Give me eight days, lass. And no more questions." Ivy watched him walk out the chamber door. She had eight days with this man who threatened to break down every wall she had built. "Eight days." She grinned and fell back onto the bed.

Chapter Eight

Ivy found her way up to the battlements, in desperate need of fresh air. Three days had passed since her agreement with Kellen. He had been making it perfectly clear that he meant business. He'd kept his distance just far enough to make her desire for him grow even more. That's why she needed to escape after the evening meal before she jumped across the table and ravished him like a wild animal.

During the meal he'd flashed her his irresistible smile that expressed more than a friendly gesture. He was waiting to execute the final move in this love game they were playing. Kellen played very well. But Ivy wasn't bound to give up the fight so easily, even though he was putting forth his best effort to break down her defenses.

Every morning he greeted her with a small basket of mistletoe and holly, and a kiss on the cheek as they went to break their fast. Since it was too cold outside, the afternoons were spent indoors. Kellen took her through the castle, showing her the many tapestries that hung on the walls, and told her the stories they portrayed. Kellen came from a long line of noble Irishmen who had settled in Scotland. When he told her that his great-grandma had been a princess of Scotland, Ivy stood in awe. As they moved from room-to-room, she couldn't shake the familiar feeling tugging at her soul. As foreign as Castle

MacLachan was, it held a warmth, a sense of familiarity that she'd been here before, which was insane.

Indeed, Kellen had been a gentleman, giving her space without pursuing her relentlessly. Though if she was honest, she missed his smoldering gaze boring down onto her, heating her to the core. She missed his lips on her skin, trailing a fire trail in their path. She missed his soft caress that made her shiver. She was losing this battle every minute she was around him. Unlike her past relationships, he gave her everything she asked for and asked for nothing in return. She'd never met a man before who she instantly felt a connection with. Why did he have to be in Medieval Scotland?

The wind blew an icy chill over her body and she pulled her cloak tight as she stood looking over the battlements into the Highlands. Fiery torches flickered and fought to stay lit on the walls. The days were shorter, leaving them in darkness most of the day and the festivities became livelier as soon as the sun faded away, which meant if she was back home, she would be sitting on her couch watching the lights on her Christmas tree flicker, recalling a time in her life she wished had never happened. It would be one year on Christmas Day since the cancer had taken her father's life. God, she missed him.

She wiped a cold tear from her cheek and inhaled the crisp, fresh air. "I miss you, Dad," she whispered.

"Och, there ye are. I was wondering where you escaped to. Ye left me trapped, listening to auld man Lamont gob aboot how he lost his right eye in battle. I've heard that story several times." Kellen chuckled then grew serious when he saw Ivy swipe away a tear with her arms folded across her chest. "What's wrong, Ivy?"

"I'm fine." She inhaled and did her best to smile. "I don't feel like celebrating tonight."

Every night since she'd been here there had been an ongoing festival. Tonight the celebration was inside the castle as clan members gathered, feasting, dancing, and drinking around a fire in the middle of the great hall. When Ivy had asked Moina why there had been gatherings every night, she replied, "'Tis the daft days before the Winter Solstice."

Kellen towered over her, wiping her tears away. "Lass, what can I do to help? I dinnae like to see ye cryin'."

"There's nothing you can do," she looked up at him. "My father passed away this time last year. I miss him." She tried to hold steady, fight back the tears, but the emotions ran too deep; she was on the edge of breaking down.

"I'm so sorry." He wrapped his arms around her and held her tight. "I know yer pain, and if I could I would take it all away."

64

Ivy sobbed. For the first time since she'd buried her father she allowed herself to succumb to the pain of her loss.

She sniffled. "Kellen, he was in so much pain." She shook her head against his chest. "And I could do nothing about it but stand there and watch him die and try to be strong for my mother."

"But ye were there for him. Ye got to say goodbye."

Ivy lifted her head and met his dark gaze. Kellen had also lost a love and he hadn't had the privilege of saying goodbye.

"You're right. I guess I didn't realize how much I've been holding in."

"Ivy, ye took care of everyone but yerself. Ye need time to grieve." Kellen exhaled and looked up into the black sky. "Bloody Hell, I sound like me brother."

Ivy smiled through her tears.

"Kellen cupped her face. "There were times I wanted to die and join me wife, but I knew she would kick me arse for such actions. She was a wee bit feisty." He winked. "I can remember taking me sons out fishing one day. Wylie must have been two summers. Me wife told me to leave the boy at home, that he was too young to play with the big laddies. Of course I sneaked him oot, and we headed to the loch. The day was beautiful and the fish were plenty. I was teaching Patrick how to fillet a fish and took me eyes off the wee one for the briefest moment and—"

"Wylie fell into the loch and almost drowned." Shocked by what she'd said, Ivy covered her mouth with her hand. *Where did that just come from?*

Kellen paused and looked at her with suspicion.

Ivy scrambled to find the words to explain, but she had no idea what had just happened; it was as if she'd watched the whole scene play out right in front of her. "A good guess, huh?"

"Aye, I would say so." He smirked. "That night I slept wit' the dogs."

Ivy laughed, trying to draw attention away from what had just happened.

"Now, ye try it. Tell me something ye remember aboot yer Da."

Ivy exhaled and tried to focus on what Kellen was asking, but her mind kept replaying that tragic scene. Her body tensed and her heart beat to a panicked rhythm, as if she was reliving that moment. *Focus Ivy.*

She cleared her throat. "Every Christmas it was a family tradition that my dad and I would go to a place where you cut down your own Christmas tree. Before you came out, I was looking at that fir tree over there," she pointed, "it reminded me of my dad."

Kellen looked puzzled. "Ye cut down a tree, and then what do ye do wit' it?"

"We would put the tree in a stand and bring it into the house to decorate. That's where we would store gifts for our family and friends until Christmas Day. It's a tradition where I come from."

"I see."

A cold breeze blew across them and flurries began to fall. Ivy shivered.

"Lass, let me escort ye back inside where 'tis warm."

Ivy smiled and nuzzled next to Kellen. Indeed, there was some strange magic here. Though she couldn't understand it, she felt it's mysterious enthralling power.

~~~~~

"What do ye mean ye haven't told her!" Donnelly blurted out.

"'Tis no' the right time. If I tell her now, she won't believe me. I won't risk losing her." Kellen sat down behind the desk in his solar, glancing at two new charters lying in front of him.

"I dinnae understand. The gods have answered yer prayers."

"Aye, but she must believe. She must fall in love wit' me all over again."

"I know, but what is to happen when time runs oot and she has yet to fall in love wit' ye? Kellen, I can no' see ye go through all this pain again. I can no' do it." Donnelly shoved his hand through his hair as he paced in front of the hearth. "I say ye bed the lass and be done wit' it. Do that trick I taught ye with yer tongue. She'll fall in love really quick."

Kellen laughed. "Och brother, I plan on doing that every night once I have her back in me bed."

He stood and walked over to Donnelly. "I can no' interfere wit' fate. If I push too hard, then I'll never see her again."

"Ye're no' pushing hard enough." Donnelly bit back.

"Did I tell ye Ivy had a breakthrough last eve?"

"Nay."

"I told her the story of when I took the lads fishing and Wylie almost drowned. She remembered it."

"So, then 'tis done. She remembers?"

"Nay, no' exactly. I think it scared her. She still doesn't understand."

Donnelly exhaled in frustration. "God's bones! We running oot of time."

Kellen placed his hand on his brother's shoulder. "I have this under control. Dinnae fash yerself."

Kellen made his way to the door, for he was done with this conversation. Indeed, he had everything under control and he would prove it come next eve. "Donnelly, be ready come early sun-break. We won't have much sunlight, so dinnae be late. Me and the boys will be in the barn waiting."

"Aye." Donnelly waved him off as Kellen shut the door.

Chapter Nine

Ivy tossed and turned most of the night with images looping through her mind. Dreams? No, they felt too real. One moment she felt like an outsider looking in on this family, as if she was watching a movie; the next moment she was the leading lady. She awoke in a sweat with labored breathing, trying to understand why she felt such a terrible loss. Was she still mourning her father that deeply?

Whatever was happening scared her. She needed to return home where her life was comfortable, predictable…alone. She needed to get back to work at the gallery. A thought struck her and she wondered if Poppy or perhaps her mother were out looking for her. No, her mother had left her the day her father died, claiming she couldn't cope with the pain. Ivy was a reminder of how much she missed her husband. Her mother had checked out long ago. Not that it mattered. No one was going to find her, because, as crazy as it sounded, she'd time-traveled back to the fourteenth century. Ivy shook her head, still baffled about how she'd gotten here. She had to find the garden again and go home to escape these images she didn't understand.

Once the sun broke, Ivy climbed out of bed, splashed her face with some very cold water, and dressed for the day. First thing she was going to find Kellen and tell him of the images she was having and demand he take her to the garden. He had to know how to find it, and if she was guessing right, he knew about the legend as well.

Ivy tied a cloak around her shoulders and quit the bedchamber. As she walked down the corridor, a baby's faint cry lured her toward a bedchamber; the door was ajar. She crept in and to her surprise Breann was fussing. Ivy looked around the room. "Moina, are you here?" There was no reply and Breann's fussing became louder.

Ivy walked over to Breann's crib where the wee one was on her knees with tears streaming down her cheeks. "Shhh." She bent down, picked the babe up and bounced her in her arms as if it was second nature, soothing and calming the child.

"You must be hungry." She looked down at the babe. Wide, blue eyes stared back at her. She gave pause when she noticed blonde curls on Breann's head, just like she'd had when she was a babe.

Ivy shook her head, which made Breann laugh. "It can't be."

She didn't know how long she had been swaying back and forth, humming a familiar yet foreign tune when Moina entered the bedchamber and paused as she saw Ivy holding Breann. "I see ye have met wee Breann."

"Yes." Ivy smiled. "She's beautiful."

"Aye." Moina walked over to a wooden chest and pulled out a small woolen tunic dress. "The laird wants us to go to the market square today and fetch some spices

71

and figs for tonight's feast." Moina took Breann from Ivy and lay her on the bed, undressing her.

"May I?" Ivy asked as she stood next to Moina, watching the babe kick her legs and fuss.

Without speaking, Moina stepped aside.

As if Ivy knew exactly what she was doing, she dressed the baby.

"Dinnae be late. We leave after ye break yer fast," Moina said, then quit the room.

~~~~~

"Patrick, a wee bit to yer left," Kellen directed.

"Da, enough. Me arms are tired from holding this prickly tree," Patrick exclaimed.

Donnelly huffed. "Yer son is right. It can no' be any straighter."

"I want this tree to be perfect, understand," Kellen stated as he stood back and observed the oversized fir tree taking up more than half the space in the corner of his great hall. "Taddy, Wylie, are the decorations finished?"

Wylie ran into the great hall with an arm full of pinecones. "Aye, Da."

Kellen bent down and took a cone from his son and nuzzled it between the full, green branches. "That'll do."

"Kellen," Donnelly said, sounding fed up with holding the monstrous tree.

"Fit for a queen," Kellen grinned.

At that moment Moina and Ivy entered the great hall, finished with their market square jaunt. Kellen stood steadfast as he watched Ivy holding Breann. If Donnelly hadn't been standing next to him, Kellen would have shed a tear. It was the most beautiful image he'd ever seen.

Ivy froze, pausing in her conversation with Moina as soon as she saw the huge fir tree.

Moina took Breann and made her way upstairs to the babe's chamber for a quick change.

"Come laddies." Donnelly gathered the boys and headed outside, but before they left Wylie ran to Ivy and tugged on the hemline of her dress, gaining her attention. "I made this for ye. 'Tis an angel to look after ye wherever ye go."

Smiling, Ivy bent down to Wylie's level and examined the cloth doll. The child was quite creative, she thought as she admired the feathers on the angel's wings. "Wylie, it's beautiful. I will cherish it always." She kissed him on the cheek. "Thank you."

Blushing, the child ran off and joined his uncle outside.

Ivy returned to the fir tree, touching its branches like she didn't believe it stood in front of her.

Kellen slid behind her and wrapped his arms around her. He pulled her closer against his body and was pleasantly surprised when she accepted his touch and leaned her head back against his chest.

"Kellen, you have no idea how much this means to me."

"Nothing could please me more than seeing ye happy." He pushed aside her cloak and kissed her shoulder. "Lass, I've done me best to be on me best behavior but ye dinnae make it easy for me."

Ivy closed her eyes, sinking farther into Kellen's embrace. "You're a hard man to resist."

He trailed his kisses up her neck. "Does this mean ye be falling in love wit' me, lass?" By the saints he prayed to Holly that she was.

Ivy reached behind her and gripped his cock. "I can't tell you all my secrets now, can I?"

When he felt her hands envelop him, it was his undoing. His resolve shattered, and raw male instincts surfaced, driving him to claim her. In one fluid motion, he shoved her sleeve off her shoulder, exposing her bare skin, then wrapped her hair around his hand and pulled her head back, giving himself more access to her neck. Once he had her where he wanted her, he devoured her skin, kissing passionately, unable to satisfy his hunger.

Relentlessly, Kellen continued kissing her, making her surrender to his touch until it wasn't enough to satisfy the growing ache inside him. He craved more. He needed more. "Ivy," he said breathlessly, "if ye dinnae want me, tell me to stop now…" He froze when he felt her hands untie his trews and slip inside. "Bloody Hell, lass."

Kellen spun her around and threw her over his shoulder. Ivy giggled.

With one arm holding her steady and his other hand gripping his trews in place, Kellen made his way to the kitchen. Nothing was going to stand in his way. He was going to claim her.

In one motion Kellen swept his arm across a table in the kitchen, clearing all its contents to the floor. He sat Ivy on top, grabbing her legs and pulling her forward. "Kellen," she said breathlessly. "Someone will see us."

"I dinnae care," he groaned against her lips and pulled her dress up to her thighs.

Ivy placed her hands on his chest and gave a little push. "The boys."

Kellen grumbled.

He searched the kitchen, but all the nooks and crannies were out in the open. Then he remembered the pantry. It had a door and was private. "Pantry, now," he demanded.

Again he picked Ivy up and she wrapped her legs around his waist as they quit the kitchen for the pantry. Kicking the door closed behind them, he left them in thick darkness. He stepped in a basket on his way to a table setup against the far wall. "Shite. I feel like a wee lad sneaking aboot. This is me home I should be able to bed me wife."

Ivy froze as Kellen set her down on the table. He hung his head on her shoulder and cursed himself for a damn fool. What was he thinking?

"Yer wife?"

Taking a step back, he ran his hand through his hair in frustration.

"Kellen, you want to explain to me what's going on here?" Ivy hopped down from the table and adjusted her dress.

Exhaling, Kellen looked up to the ceiling, wondering how he was going to explain everything to her without her fleeing back to the garden. "It was no coincidence that ye traveled back in time, Ivy. At first I couldn't allow myself to believe it but 'tis true."

Ivy stood confused. "What is true?"

"Lass, ye are me wife and we are yer family."

Ivy took a step back toward the door. "What do you mean?"

Kellen approached her, holding out his hand, trying to comfort her but she motioned for him to stop. "Don't come any closer."

"Please Ivy, I can explain." He reached into the waistband of his trews where he had sown the bundle of holly leaves he had found in her room. "Here." He handed the leaves to Ivy. "Ye wished upon them as well. Ye must know about the legend."

Ivy grabbed the bundle. "The legend is nothing more than an old folklore."

"Ye dinnae believe? Is that what ye're telling me?"

"I—I don't know what to believe." Ivy opened the door and strode to the kitchen with Kellen following closely behind. "One minute I'm walking home from my gallery, I twist my ankle, and I fall asleep in my bed then awake in a garden that I've painted."

"Then ye remember the garden?"

"What do ye mean?"

"Ivy, ye died giving birth to Breann. Me and Donnelly buried ye in the winter garden. I prayed upon the holly and ivy leaves that the Gods would bring ye back to me."

Ivy stood frozen.

"Ye must believe me. How else would ye have known aboot Wylie almost drowning in the loch?"

Ivy shook her head in disbelief. "How…did…I—"

"Part of the legend says that if ye believe in true love, yer prayers will be answered. Even though yer body died, yer soul traveled back to me. I kept faith, love. Ye were always the best part of me. I could no' lose ye…I can no' lose ye again." His voice cracked as he fought back tears.

Kellen wrapped his arms around her, holding on to hope that she would understand and come back to him.

"No, no, no." Ivy whispered and stepped away. "This is not fair, Kellen. If this is true, my soul is traveling through time, I'm living another life in the twenty-first century. I don't remember my life here."

"But ye remember me." He took her hands in his and held her gaze. "Tell me how it felt when ye held Breann for the first time. Tell me how it felt to look into Wylie's eyes as he gave you the angel he made for ye. Tell me ye dinnae remember me kiss." He cupped her face and bent down, claiming her lips. He held her tight, for he knew he would lose her if he let her go.

Ivy pulled away, shaking her head. "I don't know how to feel, I'm lost. I need air." She ran out of the kitchen and across the great hall, reaching the heavy wooden door leading to the outside bailey.

"Ivy!" Kellen called after her, but she kept running. He went after her, then stopped as she ran out the door. Their life together now lay in the hands of the Gods. He couldn't make her stay if she didn't want to. Donnelly had warned him the day he decided to bury his wife in the winter garden. There was no guarantee that she would return to him the same woman, yet it was a risk he was willing to take. He prayed he had enough faith for the both of them and that she **would** return.

Chapter Ten

Ivy had to escape this madness. None of it made sense to her, yet she couldn't shake the feeling that Kellen had been right. But it made no sense. And how? How could someone travel through time and have lived two totally different lives? *"Yer soul traveled, lass."* Kellen's words echoed through her mind. Ivy ignored them and did the only thing she could to protect herself—she ran.

Ivy raced past a group of townsfolk gathered around a raging bonfire in the middle of the bailey, celebrating the winter solstice. They danced in a circle, laughing under snow flurries. She didn't dare look behind her, for she knew she couldn't stand to see the hurt in Kellen's eyes.

Her mind was a muddled mess, not understanding how she got here or if she believed in such magic. Even though her father trusted the legend, it hadn't saved his life. As far as she was concerned, the Christmas Curse had been more believable.

The snow crunched beneath her boots as she kept running. She had to reach the garden and return home; she had no other choice. It was the one thing that made sense to her. Unfortunately, she didn't recall where the garden was located, so she could only pray that she was heading in the right direction.

Once Upon a Winter Solstice

After running for what seemed like hours, she stopped to catch her breath, and searched for some hint of the garden, but nothing looked familiar. Ivy fell to her knees defeated, and sobbed. There was no winter garden. In her hand, she squeezed the holly and ivy leaves. "Please if there is some truth to all of this, please show me the way." She looked up to the sky and prayed.

She hung her head and the snow started to glisten around her. It began in a small circle, then spread outward into larger rings until it covered the ground in shimmering tiny crystals. Ivy stood and watched as a black iron fence caged her inside. Ivy vines danced and weaved through the iron slats, and a huge holly bush burst up through the ground beside her. The wind howled, blowing the gate open. She was standing inside the winter garden.

A bright white light shined off in the distance and moved toward her. She held her hand up to block the blinding glare. Warm rays heated her body and pulled her in. Her head spun and she became dizzy.

Flashes of images flickered before her of Patrick, Thaddeus, Wylie, and Kellen and their life together. An image flashed of a blue and yellow ribbon wrapped around a man and woman's wrist with the frayed ends blowing in the wind. Flashes of each of the boy's births flicked behind her eyes. Her stomach wrenched in pain. Finally, with utter clarity, she remembered her husband and their love that ran soul deep.

"Kellen!" she called out as she fought against the pull.

The last thing she remembered was her world fading to black.

Once Upon a Winter Solstice

Chapter Eleven

In a panic, Ivy sat up in bed. Blue and gold striped drapes blew into the room, along with a gusty chill. She pulled her comforter up around her neck and exhaled, relieved she was back in her own room and in her bed, not in another, harsher time. Yet deep inside she ached with a sense of loss so deep she thought she could not bear it.

The room grew colder, too cold to stay under the covers, therefore Ivy climbed out of bed and shuffled to the window to close it. As she pulled back the curtains, she saw the sky was overcast and the ground was covered in a light dusting of snow, giving the day a heavy, gloomy feeling. Or was it the sad heaviness that weighed on her heart, as if she was missing someone—someone necessary to her soul.

"Was it all a dream?" If it was, it was the most real dream she'd ever felt, and she wanted to go back to bed and return to her beautiful fantasy. "Kellen," she whispered. She clenched her chest, trying to stop her heart from aching. She had no doubt now that he had spoken the truth. She'd seen her past life with Kellen and her children, and felt every emotion attached to it right before the white light consumed her. But it had been too late…it had taken her too long to believe in the legend…to believe in Kellen.

As much as Ivy wanted to curl up in bed to grieve for what she had only just discovered, she needed to start picking up the pieces of the time she had lost. Or had she? There was no telling how much time had passed in her world. Grabbing the little black TV remote, she turned on the cable box and flipped to the local news station. "December 22nd?" Time had stood still. It was as if she had never left, yet she knew for certain she had spent eleven days with Kellen. Ivy shook her head. This all had to be some crazy dream. She needed some fresh air and a cup of coffee.

After a most necessary hot shower, Ivy dressed in her favorite blue jeans, red turtleneck sweater, and calf-length brown boots. She blow-dried her blonde hair and applied light makeup; she was never one who wore a lot of cosmetics. Her natural beauty was enough. With one last look, she adjusted her sweater around her hips and ran her fingers through the blonde waves that cascaded down her back.

She made her way down the stairs and to the front door. Slipping on her long winter coat and matching knit hat, she grabbed her purse and opened the door. The cold air insanely stung her lungs and pricked her skin, causing her to nuzzle deeper into her coat. Indeed, she needed that cup of coffee, now.

The line at the local coffee shop had been short today. On any given day, Ivy would have waited at least thirty minutes in line. Most of the tourists had gone back home, which helped slow things down a bit, and besides, Christmas was a couple of days away.

Ivy left the shop sipping on her latte, and decided she didn't want to go home right away. The only things there were wasted memories. Across Main Street there was a huge park that had everything from a playground, a pond, picnic tables, and even a small open amphitheater for concerts and plays. In fact, Ivy normally spent her lunch breaks under a tree by the theater. It was her favorite spot.

Crossing the street, she made her way to her bench. Regardless of the gray morning, people were still strolling leisurely about, especially at the amphitheater. Ivy took a seat and watched the commotion. People were on horseback in costume. Some wore chainmail and surcoats while others were in tunics and kilts. Part of the theater was set up as a castle.

She almost choked on her coffee when she saw a small version of her winter garden with a holly bush in the middle. It was just her luck; she came here wanting to escape thoughts of her time in Scotland...forget about Kellen...forget about the ache in her chest, but now right in front of her, taunting her, was a play in progress about medieval times.

Ivy reached in her pocket and grabbed the holly and ivy leaves she'd yet to throw away. It was the one thing she had to remind her of Kellen and the children. *My children.*

A tear rolled down her cheek as she ran her finger across the holly leaf.

"Ye know the one thing that bugs me aboot these plays, is the accents. They're no' authentic."

Unaware that a man had sat down beside her until he spoke, she stood to leave, never making eye contact with the stranger. She had come here to be left alone.

"One would think they could do a wee bit of research on the winter garden and know holly always follows ivy."

Ivy froze. *It couldn't be. Could it?*

Slowly, she glanced over her shoulder and her heart flopped like a fish out of water.

Sitting on the bench: a man with long dark hair pulled back into a ponytail, wearing jeans, a white t-shirt, and a tan leather jacket, smiled at her, flashing a dimple.

"Kellen?"

The man stood and cupped her face. "Aye, lass."

"But how did you get here? In the present, I mean? I don't understand." She was afraid to believe it, in case he suddenly disappeared, just as he had that first night when she hurt her ankle. Yes, she realized all at once, that had been Kellen too! Looking out for her.

He held his own bunch of holly leaves bound by ivy. "I heard ye call out for me, right at the end, before ye disappeared from the garden in Scotland, so I followed ye. Though it took me a while to find ye, my love."

Standing on the tips of her toes, Ivy flung her arms around his neck and sobbed. "I thought I'd lost you forever."

He held her face, wiping away her tears. "I told ye, I can no' lose ye again."

"Where are the kids?" Ivy looked around the park.

"Shhh. The children are back home waiting for their mother to return. Wylie wanted me to give this to ye." Kellen reached inside his jacket and pulled out the angel the little boy had made for her.

She took the doll and more tears streamed down her face as she looked up at the man who had stolen her heart so very long ago. She smiled. "Kellen."

"Aye, me love."

Ivy met the dark depths of his eyes, knowing her soul was finally at peace. "Take me home."

THE END

About the Author

Victoria Zak is an international best-selling author of the Scottish Historical Paranormal Romance series the Guardians of Scotland. Her first book Highland Burn, was a 2015 RONE award finalist for best paranormal romance. She has also written in the World of DeWolfe Pack, Amazon Kindle Worlds, for USA Today best-selling author Kathryn Le Veque.

When not conjuring her next story, Victoria enjoys spending time with her husband and two kids.

Victoria loves to hear from her readers. You can connect with her through the links below:

Website www.victoriazakromance.com

@VictoriaZak2

https://www.facebook.com/VictoriaZakAuthor

Books by Victoria Zak

Guardians of Scotland Series:

Highland Burn

Highland Storm

Highland Fate

Highland Destiny

Hell's Cowboys Series

My Immortal Cowboy

Kiss Me Deadly (2017)

Hell on My Heels (2017)

Stand Alones

Once Upon a Winter Solstice

De Wolfe's Honor

The Jewel of Grim Fortress